White Lilies Creek

Janina Raven

White Lilies Creek

A Fantasy Thriller

Herstellung und Verlag: BoD – Books on Demand, Norderstedt
ISBN: 9783754337028

WEIRD THINGS
Sparrow

"**W**eird things are going on in *White Lilies Creek*, the village near the estate of *White Lilies Manor* which came to dubious fame almost a year ago when a teen girl was murdered. *This year's incidents seem to be connected to the same wicked magic, since the whole village, with its citizens, is slowly turning into a Victorian Era English town. So much for the news, here's the weather...*"

I stood in the doorway, petrified, staring at the little radio in the corner of the waiting room of Doctor Mortimer Morrigane's vet practice, the unicorn squirrel Rain in my hands.

Weird things. At White Lilies.

I had spent numerous nights awake, praying for the nightmare to be over. For the LeDouxes to have learned their lesson and give up their blood thirst.

But it had been in vain, apparently. Now they were back, in May 2021, almost one year after the terrifying incidents. Just last week, Thorne and I had attended our last therapy session to cope with Jasmine's death, hoping to never hear about the LeDouxes again – the news had lost interest long ago.

I dropped into a chair, ignoring the questioning looks of the other waiting people, and took out my phone to text Thorne.

I'd had to hurry on my way from my job at the bakery to be on time for my spontaneous appointment with Dad, and had not had the chance to message my boyfriend yet.

To tell him that I wouldn't make it home on time.

To tell him that I was at my Dad's vet practice to have him look at Rain.

To tell him that I had found the unicorn squirrel unconscious on a table in the bakery after my shift.

And now, I texted him to say that he should not, under any circumstances, open the door for anyone.

ANYONE
Thorne

My phone and the doorbell rang at the same time.

I hesitated, but decided to haste down the stairway to open the door – I wanted to be faster than Cecily, our old landlord from the ground floor flat, who was incredibly curious about anything and anyone who visited us. I sprinted down the stairway, past Cecily Williams' apartment, to the main entry of the old house.

Sparrow and I had moved here when we realised that the LeDoux family had erased the memories of Sparrow's existence from all her loved ones – except her parents. When the incidents at the manor had become public, everybody came to the realisation that their memories had been tampered with, but it was hard for them to comprehend. As such, we had moved in together, further away from them to ease the transition of me being back in their lives.

I arrived downstairs.

I was pretty sure it must just be Sparrow, who often forgot her keys. Without a second thought, I opened the door.

But it wasn't her. A girl, yes, a familiar face, but it wasn't Sparrow.

I froze. Looked left and right. Took a deep breath. *Hallucinations?* No, this seemed too real.

"Jasmine," I finally managed to say.

For a second, we just stared at each other. "I think so, yes," the girl in front of me replied. "Can I come in?"

"S... sure." I stepped aside to let her pass and closed the door. Taking another deep breath, I wordlessly led her upstairs. I had accidentally closed the apartment door when hasting downstairs, so we stood in an awkward silence as my shaking fingers fumbled the key into the lock. I turned it and opened the door for us to go inside.

Finally, we sat on the sofa, next to each other but still distanced.

"So, how... how come you are here?" I finally asked without making eye contact.

"I don't know." Jasmine put her feet on the sofa and wrapped her arms around her legs. "I don't know what I am doing here." She took a deep breath before saying the words that shattered my heart. "I don't even know who you are."

SLEEP POTIONS
Sparrow

"**H**ey, Sparrow, are you two okay?" my Dad asked, quickly looking at Rain and then back into my eyes when I entered his treatment room.

"*I* am," I replied. "But Rain isn't, as I told you on the phone. I'm so worried..."

"Show me," Dad said, his expression turning grave.

I handed him the small furry bundle I was carrying in my hands. He carefully put Rain down on the table before opening a drawer.

Watching him take out several instruments, I sat down on the chair in the corner. This had been my spot during my childhood, a place to observe him work any time I visited after school.

"How was your day?" Dad asked.

I let out a deep sigh. "Haven't you heard the news?"

"No." He didn't look at me, staying focused while using a stethoscope on Rain's fragile body.

"I don't know who I should worry more about," I replied, "Rain, or myself and Thorne."

Dad shook his head. "I don't know what this is about, but maybe both cases are connected?"

"Why?" I jumped up from my chair and stared at him.

"Tell me the news first," he said, taking a book from a shelf. "I quickly need to look something up, but I'm all ears."

I shed light on the situation about White Lilies Manor and White Lilies Creek, the village.

"It is turning into a Victorian city?" Dad looked up at me. "It's clear that those weird LeDoux people are involved, right?"

"Sure."

"Did anything suspicious happen to you in the last days? You know, the feeling of being watched for example?"

"I'm always watched in the bakery, so... I don't really know," I had to confess.

"Well, I found out what happened to Rain." Dad gave me a serious look. "Someone fed him a plant that is harmless to humans – it reduces stress – but for an animal like Rain, it has an effect like a sedative. This plant is called jasmine."

❧ 🕷 ❧

Thorne

"**W**hat do you mean, you don't know me?" I asked after a second of silence, still in shock.

"I don't know you, while you seem to know me." Her hand trembled when she tucked a strand of brown hair behind her ear. "I was told to pick you up and travel back with you."

"Travel?" I got up from the sofa to increase the distance between her and me. "Listen, Jasmine! You are supposed to be dead! And now, one year after this crap happened, you appear in my apartment, telling me you have to travel together with me? I'm wondering whether I've gone insane and you are just a ghost of my past, or if there is a real explanation for this!"

Her eyes glazed over. "Dead. Yes, that's what I've been told as well. Obviously, I had a life before this. But I can't remember a thing – only that I woke up in a stone circle, together with dozens of other teens, two days ago."

"Together with other teens?" My mind raced. What work of the devil was going on here?

"Yes. Okay, listen. I'm not supposed to talk. I'm supposed to take you on a journey. Here are the train tickets. Are you in?" She showed me two tickets, waiting for my reply.

"Who sent you?" I asked, even though the answer was already clear to me.

"A woman with reddish hair and a beautiful dress."

"Rosary LeDoux." My voice broke. "Jasmine, this woman is dangerous!"

"How funny." Jasmine narrowed her eyes. "That's what she told me about *you*. So, will you come with me or not?"

"Obviously not!" I wondered how much of our common past I could tell her to explain why this was absolutely not a good idea, but before I could even start, she reached for something in her pocket again. "Well, in that case, I'm supposed to show you this."

She gave me two small Polaroid pics that I stared at for some seconds, then dropped them as if I had just burned my fingers. One of them was a picture of Sparrow, working behind the counter of the bakery, with the text "We are watching you" in red letters, and the other one showed Rain lying on a table – unconscious, or even dead?

"If you want to see that thing alive again, you better come with me." Jasmine picked up the pictures and shoved them back into her pocket.

"I need to call Sparrow first," I mumbled. "Give me a second."

"No." Her hand slid into her jacket and she revealed a small pistol. "I was told that is absolutely forbidden."

And as I followed her outside, I could only wonder how that girl with a terrible crush on me had turned into a brutal marionette of my former family.

≈ 🕷 ≪

Sparrow

I felt eyes resting on me from everywhere the moment I left the bus with the slowly waking Rain in my arms. Though when I turned around, nobody was there. Had I become paranoid or were the LeDouxes really watching us? If yes – how long had they been doing that? And why? As revenge for us hurting their reputation?

Thorne hadn't read my messages yet. He usually spent a lot of time on his phone, gaming or scrolling through Instagram, so something had to be wrong here.

The weird feeling didn't lessen when I entered our apartment. Thorne wasn't there. A faint scent of perfume hung in the air... perfume that Jasmine used to apply.

I brushed away the thought.

I don't have hallucinations. There is no perfume here. I'm not paranoid.

"Thorne?" My voice echoed through the empty apartment. My phone rang. I glanced at the display and picked up. "Cecily?"

"Yes. Come down. I know what happened to Fox."

∽ 🕷 ∽

Two minutes later, I sat in Cecily's flat at the dining table.

The old woman pushed her big glasses up with her palms and cleared her throat. "I'm sorry to tell you, Miss Morrigane, but your boyfriend left twenty minutes ago, together with another girl."

I was speechless for a second. "Another girl?"

"Yes. Here's a picture." Cecily handed me her phone. "This is what I could get from the surveillance cameras in the stairwell. It's not the best quality, but maybe you recognise her?"

Yes. I recognised her immediately. But I couldn't believe it.

"Are you okay, Miss Morrigane?" She took her phone from my hands. "Can I do anything for you?"

"Yes." I took a deep breath. "Listen to me, please."

"Always, Miss Morrigane."

"This girl." My voice broke and it took me some time to form the words. "This girl is supposed to be dead. It is Jasmine DeLuna."

"The girl from White Lilies-" Cecily stopped talking when she saw me flinch.

"You did hear the news, though, didn't you?" she asked. "About the village and all?"

"Yes. Can I see the video again? I need to know if it's really her."

"Sure." She handed me the phone once more. "What do you think? What does she want from Fox?"

"If only I knew." I paused the video and zoomed in on the girl's face. The picture was only in black and white, but I could still guess that her hair was darker than mine and lighter than Thorne's, which would fit... And the freckles. The shape of her face. She looked just like when I saw her for the last time.

"That's weird," I said aloud. "She hasn't changed at all!"

"Of course she hasn't changed. She was dead for almost a year, wasn't she?"

"I don't know, honestly. I thought so, but it doesn't look like that!"

"At White Lilies Manor, everything is possible." Cecily looked me straight into the eyes. "I thought you knew that, Miss Morrigane."

☞ 🕷 ☜

Thorne

"**H**ow do you know me?" Jasmine asked when we were sitting in the train, traveling to our place of doom.

"It's a long story. You wouldn't believe me," I evaded and looked out of the window, watching the girl opposite of me through her reflection in the glass. Her appearance hadn't changed, but her way of acting had.

"We've got enough time," she replied, her voice sounding cold and curious at the same time.

"We... we used to be friends." My voice sounded weak. "When you were still alive. We spent a year together at White Lilies Manor. The LeDouxes were our host family."

"And then you murdered me."

I almost choked on my spit. "No, of course not!"

"Why should I believe you?"

"Why would you believe that I killed you? We were friends!"

"Rosary told me. And I trust her more than you." Her voice was now completely cold, freezing my heart to ice. She was just a shell, controlled by the LeDouxes. The people I once called my family now controlled the girl that I once called my friend.

"But why- I mean, what makes you trust her more than me, except the fact that you woke up on her estate?"

"The fact that my memories of White Lilies Manor and its people are stronger than those of you. To be exact, I don't have *any* memories of you."

"Wait, you remember-" I frowned. "Didn't you say...?"

"I can remember some things. Places. Stuff I must have learned at school. But no faces."

"Why didn't you tell me?"

"Because I owe you nothing."

We were silent and my thoughts wandered to the pistol in her jacket.

Of course, she trusted the memories that were the strongest. Of course those were the ones of the Manor, the place where she had died.

"The LeDouxes murdered you," I reminded her. "That's why your memories of this place are the strongest! They murdered you for a bloody rite!"

"Oh my. You are a really annoying guy, do you know that?"

"Yes. I think you've told me that in your previous life as well." I sighed.

"Didn't you say we were friends?" She frowned. "Your arguments contradict, you see?"

"We hated each other at first. But in the end, we became... something like friends. When we were in deadly danger."

"Sounds weak." She crossed her arms and looked out of the window again. "I still believe that you murdered me."

I searched for words, but soon gave up.

If only Sparrow was here.

"**Y**ou should tell your mum," Cecily went on. "Mum?" I sighed. "I don't really want her to be involved in all this as well! And her past..."

"You should tell her *because of her past*. Someone like her, who fought for the magic army in the Arcane Magic Wars, will for sure be able to help you with the LeDouxes!"

"But the Arcane Magic Wars were something completely different! The whole magic army fought illegal wicked magic back then, but what is the connection here? My boyfriend left the house together with a girl that is supposed to be dead. Okay, and? What if they return later? Then I'll just yell at them for leaving without telling me a thing and I'll have alarmed Mum for nothing!"

"Do you really think they will return?" Cecily replied, pushing her glasses up her nose again. "What would be their reason for not telling you? I think I know young Fox good enough to understand that he cares about you a lot. He would never leave you, let alone to be with someone else."

At this point, I wasn't even sure anymore. The image of Jasmine kissing Thorne back in the forest flashed through my mind. What if he had just lost interest in me?

"Morrigane, you have to tell your Mum, no matter if and how the incident will be solved. She will help you to find out if there's something dark behind it."

"You're right." I sighed. "I'll call Mum. Thanks for your help, Cecily."

Taking out my phone, I left her flat and called Mum as I made my way up the staircase.

"Hey, Birdie, what's up?" I heard the happy voice of Nevada Morrigane.

"Mum. We need to talk. Can you come over?"

"Is it about Rain? Dad came home ten minutes ago and told me about him." Her voice turned serious.

Heat of shame flooded my cheeks when I realised that I had left Rain half-awake in my flat when running down to Cecily. I rummaged through the pockets of my black denim jacket to find my keys, clamping my phone between my ear and my shoulder.

"No, it's about Thorne."

"About Thorne?" With every word she said, her voice got a more and more worried undertone. "Why doesn't he call me himself? Or speak to Cecily Williams? Sparrow? Are you still there?"

"Yes, Mum", I mumbled. "Just have to find my keys- ah, here they are." I unlocked the door, walked into my apartment and took my phone into my hand again. "Sorry. No, Thorne can't call me. He- he left his phone here! He even left his phone here, that's unbelievable! I..."

"Sparrow. Please tell me what happened. Or wait, give me five minutes. I'll come over." She ended the call and I dropped down on the sofa.

Exhausted. Tired. Annoyed that we were once again involved in a mystery connected to the LeDoux family.

Ten minutes later, the doorbell rang and I heard how Cecily opened the front door and exchanged a few words with my Mum. I heard Mum's bouncy steps coming up the stairway until she came to a stop in front of my apartment and knocked, so I went to open the door for her.

Nevada Morrigane was a young woman of 34 years, and everybody said that we looked incredibly similar. She had the same green eyes as I did, and her hair was blond like mine. But way more prominent were probably the freckles on our noses and the pointy chin – and the slightly arrogant look in our eyes that neither of us had on purpose.

In her younger years, at 16 and 17, she had fought in the Arcane Magic Wars, fights that mostly happened underground – in catacombs, where old sorcerers and witchers performed wicked magic rites. Mum and the other members of the magic army had prevented these rites from affecting normal people, by arresting or even assassinating the resisting magicians.

My mum had been a famous assassin back then and her name – her real name as well as her alias "Nemo", Latin for "nobody" and an acronym for Nevada Morrigane, – was still linked to the incidents back then. Since she acted on behalf of the government, she had never faced a trial or punishment for what actually was murder. According to her, those cruel magicians hadn't been human anymore, though. Now, she worked for the normal police and avoided using the name Nemo.

Back at White Lilies Creek High School, the last name and the connection to my Mum had brought me respect and fear from other students, and for a loner like me, that had been pretty nice. Some history nerds and daring students had asked me for an autograph of my mum, but they never received one. Because I never returned to school from the summer holidays.

"Hey, Birdie. What happened?" Mum sat down beside me. Tears rolled down my cheeks as I searched for words to explain what had happened. Once again, I realised that my mother was one of the few people I could be myself around– the others were Dad and Thorne.

She wrapped her arms around me and pulled me closer to her body, a strand of hair that had escaped her chaotic bun tickling my nose.

"Thorne," I eventually mumbled. "He left without telling me. Together with Jasmine."

"Jasmine?" Mum carefully pushed me back to look into my eyes. "Are you talking about Jasmine DeLuna?"

"Yes. Cecily has a video of the surveillance cameras. It's her. She's alive again."

"White Lilies Manor really is a wild place. Now people are coming back to life there, and I'm not even surprised. But why did Thorne and Jasmine leave without telling you?" Mum frowned. "You didn't have an argument, did you?"

"No. I texted him when I was at Dad's with Rain, to tell him about the incidents in White Lilies Creek, and he didn't even read that message. When I came home, he was already gone. With her."

Rain, hearing his name, hopped onto the sofa – still slightly dazed from the jasmine flowers.

"I think it's clear that all this is connected, right?" Mum asked. "Rain – drugged with jasmine flowers – and the change of the village into a Victorian city, and the sudden reappearance of Jasmine."

"And if that's the case? What are you planning to do, then?"

Mum took a deep breath. "I'll talk to Mortimer. And then I'll get some time off from work. You should sleep a bit now, Birdie, or pack some things. We'll meet again at midnight and take the car. The sooner we get there, the better."

The first thing I realised after she spoke was the fact that it was already late in the evening.

The second thing was the fact that she wanted to travel to White Lilies Creek.

ও 🕷 ৎ

Thorne

Jasmine and I left the train at White Lilies Creek Central Station.

"Don't even attempt to flee," Jasmine said and once again, I was shocked by her cold tone. But what shocked me more was what I saw when we left the building.

All the houses in front of us that had been modern concrete constructions when I had last seen them, had now turned into smaller wooden cottages or huger stone buildings – all in the Victorian style.

"What is going on here?" I asked Jasmine.

"Don't know why I should tell you." She crossed her arms. "Let's go. I guess you know the way?"

I sighed and led the way to the estate of White Lilies Manor. We walked past many more old houses, but some streets further, as if we had passed an invisible line, the buildings were normal. Unlike in the Victorian quarter, a thick layer of fog covered the sky here.

I didn't dare to ask Jasmine again.

Was this magic or were the locals just tired of living in 2021 and changed their houses and style back to the 1800s?

We walked along the path to the estate and through the gate that I had lived behind for so long and that I had hoped to never cross again. Now I was back, forced by a former friend and my former family who had threatened to do something to Sparrow and Rain. Wait – did they even have him? Or had they just poisoned him? I didn't know. The only thing I knew was that I was back.

☘ 🕷 ☙

Jasmine

Once we were inside the manor, I led Thorne along the familiar way to the dining room, where we found the whole family sitting at the giant table. At the sound of our entrance all heads turned at once, eyes falling upon us.

I cleared my throat and announced, "I found the murderer."

They said nothing. They never said any unnecessary words. And I was okay with that – I'd never been one to talk a lot either, as far as I could remember.

"I am not your murderer," the boy next to me said insistently, and something about his expression made insecurity bubble up in my stomach, but I pushed it away. *Insecurity makes people weak,* Rosary LeDoux had told me nearly every hour since my return. *We do not want to be weak. We want to be strong.* I had never questioned what they had told me, so I didn't know what it was that made me ask, "Is that true?"

"Yes," Rosary LeDoux said with a vacant face. "It wasn't him. He was supposed to die as well. Just like Sparrow Morrigane. But they tricked us."

"Tricked you?" I felt dizzy when the pieces of the puzzle fell together. "So you..."

"I was the one who killed you. Who also destroyed your magical bond to make sure you wouldn't remember him. You know, you could also say that I was the one who stabbed you to death with this beautiful knife," Rosary said and almost softly ran her hand along the blunt side of the blade in her hand.

Then, she stood up in one fluent motion, her black dress swaying around her ankles as she neared me, seemingly levitating above the floor. The long knife in her hand was still bloody from the meat she had just cut for dinner – and if I didn't want my blood to be added to it again, there was just one choice left.

I turned around and ran.

Sparrow

After Mum had left the flat, I sat on the sofa for some time, caressing Rain's fur and staring into the void.

What if Thorne and Jasmine had just left to go out for the night? What if there was nothing behind it? What if they would return later?

What if our journey to White Lilies Creek would be in vain? Or even worse, what if we would get caught up in the mystery and put our lives on the line?

Someone knocked at the door. "Miss Morrigane?"

"Cecily? You can come in." I watched the old woman enter the flat.

"Is your Mum still here?" she asked and when I shook my head, she added, "What have you two planned?"

"She wants to travel to White Lilies Creek in about an hour," I said, "to see what is going on. You know, the village turning Victorian and all."

Cecily nodded and sat down beside me. "You know, I thought about what you said. That you don't want her involved in all that. But maybe it's time that I tell you something about Nemo's past."

"Her name isn't Nemo," I replied. "Not anymore!"

"In the context of this story, it is. Nemo and I, we worked in the magic army together. She is the best fighter I've ever met — for both assassinations and battles. If there is one person who can protect you and herself, it's Nevada Nemo Morrigane."

"You know Mum?" I blinked at her. "I have to confess, I've never seen this fighter in her, this reckless murderer. She has always been the loving Mum. And still, I can imagine her successfully fighting the whole LeDoux family alone. I think you were right to tell me to talk to her." I forced a smile upon my lips. "Thank you, Cecily."

PLEASE DIE SLOWLY
Thorne

"**S**o why have you brought me here?" I asked when after a few seconds of silence the realisation hit that nobody was going to follow Jasmine.

Rosary smiled. "Revenge, son."

"Don't call me son." Fire flashed through my veins. "You are not a part of my family anymore! You are traitors!"

"Don't you think it's the other way around?" Rosary replied, still terribly calm. "*You* are not a part of *our* family anymore. You are alone. You left us. You are the traitor."

Those four sentences hit me harder than they should have, after all that this family had done to me. But still – Rosary was right. I had left them. In their eyes I had betrayed them. I had refused to take part in the rite.

"So what's your goal?" I repeated. "Why can't we just go our own ways – you go yours and I go mine?"

"Because our ways, as different as they may seem at the first glance, are linked forever. Whatever you do, however you try to leave us, you will always end up here again. So why not just keep you here? Or end it all? The choice is yours. Play the game with our rules, or die at Summer Solstice this year."

I took a deep breath, my gaze skipping between the door and the family.

"Don't even try," Clarisse said from the end of the table. Her voice was rough as always. "You'll be dead before you even reach the door."

I raised my eyebrows and looked around the room. My eyes met the huge stone statues – there were five of them, tall faceless figures in long hoods, and every single one had a drawn bow in their hands.

"Exactly." Clarisse nodded. "The arrows are poisoned. No matter which ways you choose to get to the door, they will hit you. On my command, they will release their arrows. So you'd better listen."

"Alright." After more than two hundred years of living with them, I knew when they were serious about something. So I stayed where I was, my hands hidden in my pockets to cover up the trembling. I gave Rosary a nod, signalling her to continue.

"Have a seat." Clarisse pointed to the empty chair next to her and with legs like pudding, I walked over to her and sat down. The tips of the arrows followed me through the room.

"Here, have a drink." She poured some red liquid into my glass. It looked like wine. With a critical look to the arrows that still pointed towards me, I took a sip.

Sparrow

I walked over to Mum's house, my backpack full of things I might need later, and Rain on my shoulder.

My parents lived only one street away, so it didn't take us long to arrive. Dad was already standing in front of the door, looking out for me and waving when he spotted me.

We went inside together and he closed the door behind me, then he followed me into the living room.

Mum looked up from her phone. "There you are, Sparrow."

"Yup." I shoved my hands into my pockets. "What are you doing?"

"Just texted my boss. I'm off work for the next few days. He said it's okay because it's for a good cause – nobody else from the police dares to travel there, after the horror media articles last year."

"Nobody even attempted to catch the LeDouxes after all!" I replied.

"That's our job now." Mum stood up. "Come with me, Sparrow."

"What...?" I followed her into the hallway, stepped over one of our cats that was sleeping on the tiles, and followed Mum through an armoured door. The door to her gunroom.

As a child, the chamber had always fascinated me. It is always the forbidden things that fascinate little kids.

There were showcases full of knifes, daggers and swords; on the shelves on the walls were vials filled with poisons, acids and herbs.

Mum opened the padlock of the big safe next to the door. Dozens of different shooting weapons lay there as if on an advertising table, and on the lowest shelf were big metal boxes full of ammunition.

Mum hesitated for a second, her eyes scanning every single weapon, then she took a small revolver and placed it in my hands. "Take this. You will need it."

I stared at the weapon. As a kid, I had always dreamt of being an agent like Mum, striving for a better world. Especially when she had secretly taken me to the shooting range of the police training station to teach me how to use a gun. But now, the weapon lay heavy in my palms. And I knew what Mum's next words would be.

"Promise me to use it if it's necessary."

I didn't answer. I was pretty sure that I could never fatally injure someone – no matter who it was. No matter what that person had done to me before.

"Promise it," Mum repeated. "I couldn't live with the knowledge that you died because your heart was too good."

"Alright." I took a deep breath. "I promise to shoot whoever I need to if there is no other possibility."

Mum sighed and caressed my hair. "Good. Let's go."

She reached for a box of ammunition and two more guns and closed the safe again, walking over to the blades. "Here, take this as well." She gave me a dagger and a longer sword and put another two into her backpack. Lastly, she walked to the vials. She spent five minutes just staring at every single one, then picked a few, wrapped them into thick fabric and put the parcel into her backpack as well.

"Say goodbye to Dad and go to the car. I'll be there in a minute as well."

Dad was already waiting for us in the hallway. I gave him a hug and he said, "Good luck, Birdie."

"Thanks, Dad." I sighed and left the house, sitting down on the stairway in front of the door.

"If you don't get any sign of us in the next 24 hours, please alarm my boss," I heard Mum whispering to Dad. "But whatever you do, don't follow us. Carry on with work. Just please don't try to help up."

"But, Vadie..."

"No, Mort. One of us has to stay here and take care of the house and the cats. I don't want the same things to happen to you like in the war. You've struggled with your trauma for long enough." Mum's voice gave me the creeps. She had never talked much about the wars.

The door opened and Mum stood behind me. "You were supposed to go to the car, Sparrow."

"Why?" I replied. "Why don't you want me to hear what you said to Dad? I know that there is the possibility that we don't return! That we die there! That he might be the only one that's left of the Morrigane family!"

"It's not only about that, Sparrow." Mum led me to the car and we threw our backpacks into the trunk, went to the front and sat down.

"What is it about, then?" I asked while she turned on the engine and steered the car on the highway.

"It's about the war. About the things Dad and I experienced there."

"What were these things? Mum, don't you think I'm mature enough to know?"

"Probably." Mum sighed and paused, and right when I wanted to ask her to explain, she went on. "You know, when Mortimer and I were 15, we quit school to join the army. We already were a couple back then, and that didn't change in the time of our training there. But while Mort went to the medical unit, I became a part of the assassins. And at one point, some soldiers of the medical unit were kidnapped by some of the so-called Wicked Magicians, or just Wickeds. Mortimer was one of the kidnapped ones. It was my fault. I was the one to convince him to become a part of the army and I was also the one who had been supposed to guard our lair that night – but I sneaked away to help another unit to attack a group of Wicked Magicians. The only reason why I didn't get fired after that incident was because I was very successful in said attack unit, and because I freed the kidnapped medicals unit members all alone."

It was silent in the car and Mum turned up the volume of the music. Loud guitar riffs hit my ears and numbed my thoughts. We drove towards the rising full moon and I felt my eyelids getting heavier and heavier, until I couldn't keep them open anymore.

When Rain woke me up by biting my ear, we had already left the highway.

Mum steered the car through the abandoned streets of small villages.

"It's not far anymore," she said when she realised that I was awake.

"Why did you send me to White Lilies Manor?" I asked, turning down the volume of the music.

Mum gave me a side-glance and sighed. "You mean, how could I send you to a host family of Wicked Magicians? You might not believe it, but I didn't know about it. They did the advertisement with another name. Not LeDoux, but... Holmwood, if I remember right."

"The original last name of Rosary and Thill," I said, watching a forest area pass by outside the car. "They aren't LeDouxes, actually, but they want to be a part of that family, so they use the name of Clarisse, Kyle and Estelle."

"And to be honest," Mum continued without reaching to what I said, "I wasn't even sure if the legendary LeDoux family really existed. Back in the army, some people said their existence was just a myth. A legend, invented by the other Wicked Magicians."

"Oh." We were silent again and Mum pointed to the town sign. Some letters were missing, so it read:

Welcome to White Lilies Creek.
Please d i e slowly.

"We're here," Mum said and parked the car near a huge Victorian house. "Let's bring our things into our hotel room and then investigate this case, up at the Manor!"

"Hotel? You booked hotel rooms?"

"Of course!" Mum smiled, but it was a nervous smile. Her face was just as white as the fog surrounding us.

୧୭ 🕷 ୧୭

Jasmine

single magpie flew across the night sky as I
was on my way to leave the estate. Why did
this feel so familiar – running towards this
gate, hoping nobody would catch me? The closer I came to
the brass gate, the stronger grew the feeling– and then, as I
stumbled outside onto the path, it just disappeared.

Eventually, I stopped, gasping for air, turning around to
see if someone was there. No, I was alone. Why didn't the
LeDouxes follow me? What was their plan for me – now
that I had discovered their lie?

And what of the things that Thorne had told me was
really true? *We used to be friends.* Me and that arrogant
idiot, *friends?* But – who had *I* been in my former life?
What if I had been an arrogant idiot as well? *Birds of a
feather flock together.*

I walked on.

Maybe I would find out one day.

Maybe I wouldn't, because the LeDouxes would kill
Thorne and it was my fault because I didn't help him.

Who knew?

୧୭ 🕷 ୧୭

few minutes later, I reached the town. Slowly,
the guilty conscience inside of me became
stronger and I played with the thought of

turning around and finding out what had happened to Thorne.

I had been dead once, and even though I now had no more memories of that time, I was sure that there were worse things than being dead – and since I had nobody here, it didn't matter anymore. Or – wait, no! Didn't I have a family as well?

I stopped walking, right behind the border of the village, in between all the Victorian houses.

Two people came walking towards me and I hid around the corner of a house, watching them pass me by. Shadows covered their faces and I could only see sharp silhouettes in the moonlight, but they looked really similar. At first, I thought that they were twin sisters, but then I saw that the one was about double the age of the other. Mother and daughter, possibly.

They went the way I had just come, up to the Manor. And they didn't look like LeDouxes.

They would see what had happened to Thorne.

Problem solved.

And with a smile, I walked on, towards the train station, to find a place to sleep in the arrival hall. Tomorrow I would look up other people with my last name to find my parents.

My hand ran along my neck to find my necklace – a gesture I always made when I was nervous. But nothing was there. I had lost my necklace – the only thing that had a value to me because my full name was carved into the heart-shaped pendant.

THE ASSIGNMENT
Thorne

My tongue felt funny and I snickered every time it didn't obey me, forming different words than those on my mind.

I leaned back in my chair and watched how Estelle and Thill left the room to care for my brother. My parents were still here, as well as my grandmother, and they were all watching me, but I didn't really mind.

"You know, Son, it was all just a misunderstanding," Mother finally said, while Grandmother refilled my glass.

"A mist- missing- misunderstanning, yapss." I nodded heavily. "Dinn't expect anything else from y'all!"

I reached for my glass, but it moved, slid away from me and I needed several attempts to catch it and bring it up to my lips. The bittersweet taste of the red wine filled my mouth and with every sip, I felt warmer and fluffier.

"You know, you should have told us," Mother continued. "About this boy. What was his name, again?"

"Hmmmmh?"

"Your, uh... *friend*. The reason why you ran away."

"Ev...ie. Everesht." I blinked a few times.

"Everest, yes." Mother put her hand on my shoulder. "You could have told us."

"Toldcha what?"

"What was going on between you. You know, I caught you kissing on the Crow Tower."

"Kiss'n? Uh, righty. I'm bisex'ual. Dinn'I mention?"

I leant my forehead against the glass window of the Manor's dining room.

"Are you okay?" Mum asked, taking one of the earphones of the listening device out of her ear.

"Sure." I copied her move, my hands trembling. "Sure, just – why didn't he tell me? He always said Everest was just a friend! How come he doesn't trust me with that information? I'm queer as well, and he knows it!"

"What?" Mum turned to me and I bit my tongue when I realised what I had said. Heat rose into my cheeks. "I'm asexual. I don't experience sexual attraction. I don't look at people saying *Oh wow, I wanna fuck that person!*"

"Sorry to interrupt you, but this is not the occasion for a coming-out speech, Birdie!" Mum put her earphones in again and pointed to the dining room.

"We support you, whatever may happen," Rosary said in this second. "You should've told us, and we would have left Everest alive!"

"Sure," drunk Thorne said. "Y'wanna tell me that's all my fault, heh?"

"Yes," Rosary said, raising one eyebrow. "It's always your fault."

"Aight – wait." Thorne blinked and sat up straight. "Whataya want from me, again?"

"Your support." Rosary shrugged. "You just need to sign this magic contract, here." She handed him a parchment roll and a quill together with an inkbottle.

"What's it 'bout?"

"Your help in family issues. I think we can rely on you, right, Son?"

"Yah." Thorne took the feather.

Mum and I exchanged terrified looks, but just as I wanted to knock on the window to get Thorne's attention, she took my hands. "There's no help for anyone if they see us!"

With a heavy heart I watched Thorne sign the contract. Pain flashed through my body when he lifted the quill from the paper, and I stumbled back from the window.

"You okay?" Mum asked, but before I could reply, I saw how her eyes widened in surprise at something behind me. Rain growled and as the pain eased, I turned around. Only to stumble back once more, against the wall of the Manor. "Jasmine?"

⇛ 🕷 ⇝

Jasmine

That's my name, yes." I lowered my head, but didn't take my eyes off the two people. "And you are?"

"Sparrow." The girl narrowed her eyes. "Aren't you supposed to know that?"

"I died. I remember nothing from my former life. But I have a photo of you." I nervously fiddled the picture of the girl behind the bakery counter out of my pocket and gave it to her. How come I hadn't recognised her before? She was the girl that I had been told to photograph as blackmailing material for Thorne – and I had also poisoned her unicorn squirrel. With a plant that shared my name.

For a second, an excuse lay on the tip of my tongue, but I decided to swallow it. As long as she didn't know what I had done, there was no reason for me to make everything more complicated.

"Where did you get this photo?" Sparrow narrowed her eyes again.

"Got it from Rosary LeDoux." I took a deep breath. "I have no idea who you are, but I guess we have to talk."

"Good idea," the woman next to Sparrow said and we shook hands with some awkward looks. "I'm Nevada. Nevada Morrigane."

Something in the back of my head told me that I should know the story behind the name, but then the thought was gone again and I didn't mind it anymore.

"You two, go talk," Mrs. Morrigane said. "I'll keep on watching what's going on here."

It was a weird feeling, following this stranger into the woods, with the knowledge that she knew me.

We sat down on the moss.

"Just in case Thorne hasn't told you," Sparrow said in a sharp voice, "we lived here at White Lilies for almost one year. The LeDouxes were our host family. And then Thorne told us that they wanted to sacrifice us for an immortality rite, so we fled into the forests, but you decided to leave us, so you tried to escape through the main gate, got caught and later murdered, while saving my life." Her voice had become softer at the end. "And I never had the chance to say thank you. Even though I'm probably supposed to say, 'Why did you do that, idiot?'"

"For you and Thorne," I replied, following an inner instinct. "Wait, why did I just say that? Are you a couple?"

"Yes."

"Wow. He didn't tell me. I don't know why I know that."

"Maybe your memory is coming back?" She shrugged. "But anyway – shouldn't we talk about the present time instead of the past?"

"Think so, yes."

"Then tell me why you are alive. Seriously, I know nothing besides that you left our flat together with my boyfriend! So what is going on here?"

"The LeDouxes brought me back to life," I started, my voice trembling. It was the first time ever telling someone the whole story. "Me and a good dozen of other teens from different time periods. Mainly Victorians, I think."

"Is that why the city is turning into a Victorian city?" Sparrow interrupted.

"I don't really know, but it's possible."

"And how did they bring you back to life?"

"By picking the lilies they planted after our deaths. One lily for every teen brought back to life."

"The lilies...?" Sparrow slowly shook her head. "So that's why– fucking hell, that's unbelievable!"

"Anyway. I remember everything, except for faces and events, from my former life – and for places, I have this vague feeling of having already been there, sometimes. Well, after some days of living at the Manor with the LeDouxes, I got the assignment to take the train over to your city to take a photo of you and to feed this jasmine flower to your unicorn squirrel–" Too late, I realised what I had said.

"So it was *you*?" Sparrow jumped up. "Damn liar! You haven't changed a single bit! You're still so selfish!"

"And you? You are immature! Why don't you just *listen* until I'm finished explaining?"

"Oh, now you're coming at me with *that* thing again?" She shook her head. "Incredible, how little you actually changed."

"I've called you immature before?"

"You used to call me hatchling!"

We looked at each other for a few seconds before bursting out in laughter.

"Then please, please, Madam, do explain," Sparrow said.

"Sure." I took a deep breath. "The LeDouxes told me that they were the good guys and that Thorne had murdered me. I was supposed to get him back to the Manor by any means, so that they could take revenge."

"They really are one raven short of a murder."

"Yes. So, with the photos of you and the unicorn squirrel, I went to Thorne – obviously, I was surprised that he knew me, and since I came back to life at the LeDouxes,

I believed them rather than him. A mistake – because when we arrived here, Rosary unremorsefully told me that *she* was my real murderer. I ran away and I have no idea what happened to Thorne."

"You're an idiot! How could you run away without looking what happened to him?"

"Before you judge me, think about what you would've done if you had been in my shoes," I replied. "Also – I'm here now, so what do you want?" I felt a bit shitty saying this since I had only returned to look for my necklace, but there was no need to tell her that.

Nevada Morrigane appeared behind her daughter. "Sparrow? You should fly up to Thorne's room. They sent him there. I'll listen to them talking a bit longer, then I'll return." She turned around and left before I could even open my mouth to ask, "And what about me?"

"You go with her. I don't need your help." Sparrow disappeared into the shadows before I could protest.

"Alright," I sighed, getting up to follow Mrs. Morrigane over to the Manor.

ARGUMENTS
Sparrow

It didn't take me too long to find Thorne's room.

It had a balcony, just like my former room, and for a second I thought about just taking a short look into that one – maybe I could take some things that Jasmine missed when she got my belongings for our escape. But then, I shook away the thought. Thorne was more important, and from experience, I knew that drunk Thorne was even more chaotic and clumsy than normally. I had never experienced him *that* drunk, though.

Looking left and right, I took a few steps forward and lifted myself up into the air. Flying was the process of convincing yourself that you are lighter than air, and it was a magic power – such as umbrakinesis, my second power. This was the one I shared with Mum, her other one had to do with herbs, potions and poisons. Two strong and useful powers for an assassin.

My Dad, on the other hand, was a healer speaking animal language – perfect for his job as a vet.

When I arrived at Thorne's window and landed on the balcony, I could see that he was lying on his bed – in his street clothes.

I knocked on the glass, harder and harder. He didn't move.

I decided to break into his room. Sliding my hand through the tilted balcony door, I opened the handle and entered the room.

"Thorne?" I slapped him.

"Lemme sleep, Sparrwh," he mumbled and I sighed. He was just asleep and drunk, not unconscious.

I left the room again, flying over to Mum and Jasmine. Mum was just leaving the dining room window, while Jasmine sat on a rock nearby, her head hidden in her hands.

"What's up with him?" Mum asked.

"He's asleep," I replied. "It's impossible to flee with him in his drunk state. I think I'll stay with him to tell him that we are here as soon as he wakes up, and then we'll flee."

"Good idea." Mum nodded and picked Rain up from my shoulder. "I'll take him with me to safety, alright? I'm going to bring Jasmine down into our hotel room. She could use some sleep. And..." She lowered her voice. "If you find her necklace, please bring it."

I understood immediately. "Is that what she came back for? A *necklace?*"

"Yes. But listen, before you yell at her – you don't have any idea what she has been through in the last days. And last year."

"And what about Thorne and me?" I replied, my voice becoming colder. "What have *we* been through? I'd go as far as to say that we had a harder time than her! And now, after running away at first, she returns, not to save Thorne, but to look for her fucking necklace? And you support that? No, thank you!" I turned around and ran, followed by Mum's slowly fading begs to listen to her.

I entered Thorne's room, hid my backpack under his bed and laid down next to him.

Maybe I could get some sleep as well.

෨ 🕷 ෴

Jasmine

"Don't – under any circumstances – open the door for anyone!" Mrs. Morrigane said, giving me a serious look.

I nodded. "Alright. I'm going to sleep anyway, so I won't hear anyone knock."

"Good. Sleep well, Jasmine." She gave me a short smile and closed the door of the hotel room behind her.

She would now return to White Lilies Manor to break into the house and look around a bit, hoping that the residents were asleep as well.

I had just laid down on the bed on the wall side of the room, when someone knocked.

Don't open the door for anyone.

I stared at the ceiling, goose bumps covering my skin. What if that were the LeDouxes who wanted to murder me once again?

I remembered the idea of searching for my family. Where were they? What were they like? And would I ever see them again?

The knocking on the door became louder. "I know that you are there, Jasmine!"

I frowned. This sounded like an old woman's voice, but not like Clarisse's. Softer, and... more understanding.

"Who are you?" I asked, plodding to the door.

"A friend of Thorne and Sparrow. My name is Cecily Williams and I am their landlord. Listen, I know who you are and that you are supposed to be dead. You can trust me."

"So you think I'll trust you just because you know about me?"

"Sparrow and Thorne trust me as well. I don't know how I can prove that, though."

"Alright, so what do you want?" I decided that talking was not the same as opening the door.

"I need to see Sparrow's Mum. You might know that she worked in the magic army in her teen years?"

"The magic army," I gasped. "Right! So that's what I know her name from!"

"Wait, you can remember things from your... former life?"

"Anything but events and faces."

"Alright. So – I need to see Nevada Morrigane. I was in the army with her, and there's an important thing I need to tell her... about the LeDouxes."

"She's up at the Manor," I replied. "Spying on them and all."

"Thank you." Steps departed and it was silent. I leant my forehead against the cold wood of the door. At least I hadn't broken my promise. I had not opened the door. Even if that meant that I hadn't seen the person outside. But if what she said was true, she would helpful to Mrs. Morrigane.

With this thought, I went back to the bed and fell asleep immediately.

Thorne

Was somebody screaming?
I opened my eyes and closed them again immediately. The bright light blinded me and caused a stabbing headache.

When I tried to move, I wasn't able to do so.

At first, I thought that I was in chains. That the LeDouxes had caught me again.

Then, the memories of therapy hit me. It was just another nightmare, and I had just gotten myself entangled in my blanket.

I realised that a warm body was lying beside me.

I opened my eyes again, covering them with my hands to keep away the sunlight that entered through the windows. The windows of... my room at White Lilies Manor? Was this another nightmare? But why was Sparrow lying next to me, then?

Sparrow!

I sat up, staring at her.

With every breath, her chest lifted and lowered. I watched her for a few seconds, until her eyelids twitched and opened.

"You awake?" she mumbled, her tender voice still sounding sleepy.

"Yes. Sparrow, what... what are we doing here?"

She sat up as well, giving me a slightly annoyed look with her sparkling eyes. "You got drunk. *Very* drunk. And I guess you did something very stupid."

"What-"

"You came here with Jasmine."

"Right." Slowly, the memories returned – up to the moment when I sat down at the table with my former family. "I know everything, except for all that happened after Jasmine fled. Wait- did you find Jasmine?"

"I'll tell you later. I think it's more important to somehow reconstruct the evening." She was all serious now, even the playful sparkling had disappeared from her eyes. "Please don't interrupt me. First: You agreed with Rosary on the fact that everything was just a misunderstanding. Then, she gave you a magic contract that you signed. And then they sent you here." She hesitated and bit her lip as if there was something else she wanted to say, and I had this weird feeling that I did not want to talk about whatever this was, so I asked, "What was this contract about?"

"Family issues." She narrowed her eyes. "I don't know more. But... I wonder what happened in between the moment *you* came here and the moment *I* came here. Technically, the first thing I heard of that conversation was that Rosary saw you kissing Everest on the Crow Tower, and that you very happily outed yourself as bisexual."

My heart skipped a beat. "I did... *what?*"

"Rosary said she caught you and him kissing on the Crow Tower. You said you were bisexual, and she said that she would accept that. And she would have left Everest alive if she had known."

I took a deep breath, but my heartbeat didn't slow down, and the words came from my mouth like a waterfall. "It's not like that! I was drunk! They numbed me and I didn't know what I was saying anymore, and, you know, I'm not~"

Sparrow jumped up from the bed. "Ah yes? Now you are lying to me! You outed yourself in front of your hated family, but you try to stay in the closet in front of me?"

"Sparrow, I~" I tried to get up from the bed to calm her down, but she pushed me back and I landed backwards on the mattress. "You're such an idiot!" she screamed.

"Listen, Sparrow, I..." I sat up again and tried to put my hands on her shoulders, but she swatted them away like flies.

"Please, listen! Don't leave me, please! I just~"

"You're such an idiot!" she repeated. "You don't trust me! Why do you think I would kick you out of the house? Why do you think I would leave you?" She dropped down on the bed, right next to me, and took a deep breath. "I would rather leave you for the fact that you don't trust me to love you unconditionally than for the fact that you are bi!" She faltered. "Okay, that didn't make any sense. I'm sorry. I didn't mean to force you to anything. I~ I was just overwhelmed by... by everything." She buried her face in her palms. "I'm sorry, really. I just thought you knew you could tell me everything. Since you know that I'm queer too."

She had told me that she didn't feel sexual attraction to anyone, shortly after we moved in our flat together. And still I had never thought about telling her about my short same-sex relationship with Everest Beckett, the fourteen-year-old boy who was the first of the rite victims that had spent time with me.

"I thought it was different," I attempted to explain. "You know, that you don't feel the urge to sleep with anyone and that I fall in love with boys as well. It's something different, you understand? Especially for people of our age. Having sex isn't really important at our age, at least not for me, but romantic relationships are..."

"Yeah, I guess I know what you mean." She stared at the floor, then she lifted her gaze and looked right into my eyes. "I still love you. You should know that."

"I love you too," I replied and it was silent for a second. Then, the door slammed against the wall.

Jasmine

When I woke up, I was alone.

Mrs. Morrigane wasn't there – but wasn't it already morning? Did she really spend all night in the Manor? Or had she slept in the woods? And how had we all been able to enter the estate without being seen? Was it because the whole family was having dinner and nobody was paying attention to the entrance? Or... *had* they maybe seen us?

And what was I supposed to do now? I had been so sure that she would tell me more in the morning! But now I was alone, and I had two options. Going up to the Manor, or staying here to find out more about my parents. And I knew exactly which option sounded better. So I got up, went to the bathroom and then made my way downstairs to the hotel lobby to find a telephone book or a PC with internet access.

The porter told me that the only free PCs were in the library, so I decided to have a quick breakfast in the dining room. With a sandwich and a cup of tea, I sat down at a small table and watched the other guests while eating.

The people – tourists from different countries, apparently – chattered in many different languages and it took me a moment to understand that they had all come here for the Victorian village that White Lilies Creek was slowly becoming. Indeed, here and there people even wore Victorian dresses and suits – were those the hotel employees? While looking around further, I realised that even the hotel hall had a slightly Victorian touch – the dark wood decorations and furniture looked older than the rest of the hotel.

And this was connected to the LeDouxes bringing me and the other teens back to life.

Thorne and I watched in shock how the whole LeDoux family entered the room.

"Did we disturb your discussion?" Estelle asked from the back of the group, but Thill interrupted her before she could even finish the sentence. "No, fool. Look, they're just sitting there."

"Could you please shut your mouths, guys? Thank you." Rosary stepped forward to part from the rest of the group. Surprisingly, she didn't have the carving knife in her hands. What was she going to do? Strangle us with her bare hands? Throw us out of the window? Ah, no, she probably knew that I could fly.

"Good morning."

Huh? I had expected anything but that.

"Did you sleep well? Son, do you have a hangover?"

Thorne and I exchanged some confused looks. "Yes. But not too bad."

"Then come on, have breakfast with us!"

What kind of flashback dream was this? It was almost like back then, when we hadn't known about their terrible intentions – except for the fact that I had never argued with Thorne about sexualities or about anything in general, and that they had never come to wake us up with the whole family.

"You might be confused," Rosary said, "but we decided to give it another try. To get Thorne back into the family and you as well, as my future daughter-in-law."

I shivered at the thought of her as my mother-in-law. She was the worst possible one.

"And you think we'll get involved with you, again?" I replied. "I think you prove that you have nothing but bad intentions!"

"That was a misunderstanding," she repeated. "We'd like to start again all over, you know?"

"Sure." I frowned. "But I don't think that Thorne and I want that!"

Rosary turned around to the others, who gave her a quick nod. She shrugged and faced us again. "Then we have to do this in a different way." And there it was again, the long carving knife. I had almost even missed it a bit.

JOURNEY
Sparrow

Not even five minutes later, we sat in the dining room of the Manor, eating bread and drinking coffee.

"Here's the plan," Rosary said, unfolding a huge map of Great Britain and Europe. "You will go to this school here, see that? There, in the South of England. It's a school for magically gifted children. You will pick two very gifted ones and tell us their names."

"And then kidnap them? And their school is far away so that the traces don't lead to you again – because there is a huge distance between that school and the Manor?" Thorne added.

"Clever boy." Rosary smiled, but there was no joy in her smile.

"And you use all the other resurrected teens for similar purposes?" I added. "To send them to other schools and make them kidnap magic teens for you?"

"Exactly. Their dead blood doesn't help us anymore, so we need to get fresh blood. And for you – you haven't died yet, but for the sake of the family, we decided to give you a second chance to help us."

"Is that really the only reason?" Thorne narrowed his eyes.

"Yes." Rosary nodded and I had the uncertain feeling that she wasn't lying. What if it really meant something to her? *Family.*

"So, your train will leave in ten minutes. Take these wristbands." Before we could resist, she clicked two metal straps around our right wrists. "These will prevent you from running away." The seriousness had disappeared from her look and made place for the evil, creepy sparkling that I was used to by now.

∾ 🕷 ∾

Jasmine

"My name is Jasmine." I had practised that sentence in my mind for hours, but when I finally said it aloud to the person on the phone, I had no idea what it would mean.

"Jasmine?" The woman's voice was trembling. "I- I don't know somebody of that name."

"You do," I replied – my voice was shaking as well. I was one hundred percent sure that I was talking to my mother. "I am your daughter. I am alive."

Click. She had hung up.

DeLuna, Salena. My index finger ran along the PC screen again to find her number. Retyping the digits, I wondered what to tell her this time.

But she didn't even let me speak. "You again? Leave me alone!" *Click.*

Again, I typed the digits into the phone that I had borrowed from the friendly businessman reading a fantasy book on a sofa, somewhere between the high library shelves.

"Listen to me, please, Momma," I whispered before she could hang up again. For the second of silence, I felt cold. Had I even called her Momma? Or Mum? Mother? Salena, even?

"Jasmine," she finally said in a hoarse voice. "Prove that it's really you!"

"Magic makes everything possible," I replied. I couldn't really think of anything to say to prove that it was really me – since I didn't remember a thing from my former life. So, technically – was it even me?

"Yes," Momma said in a relieved voice. "You always said that as a child! Even when you didn't have your powers yet!"

"But... Momma, I have to tell you something," I said. Better now than later.

"Sure, Jassy! What is it?" Her voice trembled again, this time in excitement.

"I can't remember events and people from my life."

It was silent for a terribly long time.

"I will help you. I will help you get your memory back. Just... where are you right now?"

I sighed. "At White Lilies Creek. And I don't think I can return to you in the next hours."

Sparrow

Rosary and Kyle escorted us to the train station of White Lilies Creek. On the way, I secretly looked out for Mum, but she wasn't there.

Nowhere to be seen. Well, she had probably returned to the hotel for the night, right?

Almost the whole village had turned Victorian by now.

"What's this house?" Thorne asked in this moment, pointing to a huge building.

"That's the opera! Formally a motion-picture theatre, now it turned back into what it is supposed to be!" Rosary said, melancholy filling her voice and gaze.

"A motion-picture theatre? Do you mean..."

"A cinema," Thorne completed and nodded.

"There was a cinema in White Lilies Creek, and we have never been there?" I mumbled.

"Yes." Thorne shrugged. "I prefer books, honestly."

"Be silent, now! Here are your train tickets. You will not leave until the train stops at this station, and there an ally will explain you how to go on." Kyle held the door open for us and we entered the building. The two LeDouxes led us to a train that was already waiting in the station, then they watched us get on before turning around and leaving.

"They left?" I asked, turning to Thorne who had just dropped down on a free seat.

"Yes. Try to leave the train and you will know why."

"What do you mean...?" I stretched my foot towards the door and stepped forward. Forward and forward, until the metal wristband crossed the door. Pain flashed through my body and I couldn't suppress a scream.

Thorne hadn't even gotten up from his chair, but a worried shimmer lay in his glance when he frowned and turned to me. "You see? That's the thing about the metal. When I still lived with them, Rosary and Clarisse taught me some simple alchemical tricks, and this metal for example is bewitched with alchemy. When I signed the contract, those wristbands were activated to make sure we will keep the promises. We can't leave the route they have planned for us. There is no chance."

"But- It wasn't too bad," I replied. "I'm sure I could get used to it at some point."

"You think so, yeah. But the constant pain steadily increases your adrenaline level, which might cause heart problems or a coma, leading to your death." He gave me a serious look and gently put his hand on my cheek. "And we do not want to risk that."

"No." I took a deep breath. "They seem pretty thin; can't we just try and cut them?"

"You don't happen to have scissors or a pocket knife with you, do ya?"

"Sure." I reached for my pocket knife in my denim jacket.

"Great! Sparrow, you're a genius!" Thorne grinned, but worries still filled his eyes when he attempted to cut my metal wristband. He failed, slipping off and almost cutting my skin.

"Aw, crap! I'm sorry!" He handed me the knife. "It doesn't work. And apparently, it's better if I stop." He gave me an awkward grin, his hand caressing my arm.

"But-"

"We'll try and find a solution before we meet the ally."
Thorne pulled me down onto the seat next to him. "Now
please tell me why you are here, even though I had no
chance to tell you about Jasmine. Oh my, do you even
know everything about Jasmine?"

"I do." I sighed and started to tell him what had
happened since I had discovered that Rain had been
poisoned.

❧ 🕷 ❦

The train stopped at our destination: South
Farringdon Train Station.
"We should get off," Thorne said and we left the
train. Standing in the huge hall, we looked around for the
ally, but nobody came over to us.

Until an old woman approached.

"Cecily? What the hell are you doing here?" I asked.

Our landlord smiled. "Rescue you. Since you
apparently can't do that yourself."

"What do you mean?" Thorne frowned.

"Well, I have the key to free you from these terrible
chains!" She held up a thing that looked like a basic tin
opener, put it on my wristband and within seconds, the
metal clanked on the stone ground. She did the same to
Thorne, before we could even ask where she came from.
And when we did, she told us a story I could hardly believe.

"I think I told you that I was a part of the army, together
with your Mum, right? And I was an undercover spy, every
now and then visiting the LeDouxes... They thought I was

one of them, an immortal from another part of the country. And they never found out the truth, so yesterday evening, after you, Thorne, had already gone to sleep, I talked to them and asked if I could in any way help them. They agreed and sent me here."

"That's awesome!" Thorne smiled. "You're an angel, Cecily. So let's take the train back home and show the LeDouxes that they should never mess with us, for we are stronger and won't be their slaves!"

Though I thought that he was exaggerating, I felt the same rush of happiness and adrenaline in my veins. We were free now, so we could just take the next train home!

"Well." Cecily lowered her head. "There's another thing that you should know. About your Mum, Sparrow."

"Yes...?" The adrenaline rush faded, being replaced by a hollow feeling of concern.

"They caught her spying. She's their prisoner. I guess they want to blackmail you in case you won't obey."

"Oh no!" Tears stung in my eyes and I tried to hold them back. "But... you have a plan, don't you?"

"Yes." Cecily looked around in the overcrowded hall. "Let's talk later in the train. The next one back to White Lilies Creek leaves in two minutes already."

CECILY'S PLAN
Thorne

"You see, the LeDouxes are planning a huge event in the opera of White Lilies Creek, trying to get the Victorian inhabitants on their side. The more people that are on their side, the stronger they will be if there is another war."

"Another war?" Sparrow interrupted. "Do you think that it will happen?"

"Who knows?" Cecily sighed. "The LeDouxes are preparing an army. They were in the media last summer and if they do another rite this year, they will be in the media again. No matter where children disappear and are forgotten, everybody will think of this one wicked family from White Lilies Creek. And eventually, there will be someone daring to fight them."

"You mean, the teens that we and the others are supposed to choose aren't... victims but fighters?" I asked.

"Yes. They didn't tell you the truth back in the manor in case you would somehow manage to flee during the train ride, but the truth is what I was supposed to tell you: You should try to find some teens that strive for power or immortality. Those who are bullied and want to take revenge, for example."

"But that really means that they will have a small army," Sparrow replied in shock. "If every of the dozen of resurrected teens gets two magically gifted ones, that's 24! Adding the teens to this, it's 36! Plus the LeDouxes themselves and those allies that they might win from this event in the opera!"

"Exactly." Cecily took a deep breath. "That's why we have to stop them."

"And how? In disguise, just like the last time?" Sparrow rolled her eyes.

"Yes. Just that your disguise must be *better*. And I will help you. We have the advantage that you don't have to look like somebody they know – you just have to look like somebody they *don't* know. But I don't think it will be a masquerade, this time. So that might be a problem..." She sighed. "The rough plan is that we will sneak into that event with lots of weapons, and then we will free your Mum using the surprise effect!"

"And when is this event going to happen?" I asked.

Cecily sighed. "Tonight."

ↀ 🕷 ↁ

We tried to get more information from her during the train ride, but Cecily didn't want to tell us more about her plan.

"The less you know, the less you can say if the LeDouxes give you a truth potion," she said, and since we didn't know what to say, we arrived in White Lilies Creek in silence.

"You have a hotel room, right?" Cecily said when we stood in the train station hall, and Sparrow nodded. "Jasmine is there too."

"Then let's go there and ask her if she wants to support us or if she would rather leave."

For a moment, the question why she should leave when we were a team lay on my tongue, but I slowly realised we weren't a team. Never had been. We had been nothing more than a bunch of teenagers thrown into a life-threatening situation. And she had left the group.

"Yeah, let's do that."

"Wait." Cecily raised her hand. "I will go. And you will sneak into the Manor to get some Victorian clothing. And then we will meet in the hotel."

"Back into White Lilies?" Sparrow wheezed.

"Yes. I don't know which online shop will deliver some cheap Victorian clothing on time." Cecily looked around and lowered her voice, even though there were only few people around. "But I know that the whole LeDoux family is currently busy preparing the Opera! So you shouldn't be in danger."

"Good to know. Then let's hurry!" Sparrow grabbed my sleeve. "We are going to get three costumes, just in case Jasmine wants to stay. And you, Cecily, as a spy you probably have your own clothing, right?"

Cecily nodded, gave us another serious look and then left the hall.

"Then let's go." Sparrow took my hand and we made our way through the Victorian village up to White Lilies Manor.

∾ 🕷 ∽

Sparrow

I think we should go through the secret tunnel," I said when we stood in front of the wide open brass gate.

"You don't trust Cecily's observations?"

"I don't trust anyone except for my parents and you, Thorne. And after all, what if one of them realises they forgot their sacrificial knife up in White Lilies and then comes to get it and sees us stealing clothes?"

"You're right." Thorne hesitated. "Then let's hurry. How did you and Nevada get onto the estate unseen?"

"With our powers. Umbrakinesis. Mum has it as well."

"Not bad." Thorne smiled. "I don't think we need that this time. Even if someone sees us, they won't look for us in the clothing chamber, will they?"

"Don't think so." I took his hand again and we ran through the gate, towards the graveyard.

Memories flashed through my mind. How we, not even a year ago, had run the same way to rescue Jasmine, unsure if she was even there. How she had died that day, trying to save us.

I shook off the memories. We were here and alive. And we were going to rescue Mum.

Thorne and I removed the slab from a tomb to uncover the secret entrance to the tunnel, then hasted down the stairway into the dark.

Five minutes later, we stood in the torturing chamber.

"Let's hope Cecily was right," Thorne said. "We're lost if they find us!"

"I've got weapons," I realised. "They're in the backpack under your bed upstairs! Let's get them as well!"

"Weapons? You brought weapons?" Thorne frowned.

"My mum made me. She didn't let me go without. And, you know, it makes me feel safer."

"You can't kill them with mortal weapons, Sparrow, they will be alive again almost immediately." Thorne's voice sounded hoarse. "The LeDouxes are different to anyone your Mum has fought in the wars. Not many Wicked Magicians strived for immortality. They sought vengeance for crimes or tried to heal their wounds, and some attended the rites every second or third year or even fewer, but nobody has been immortal and ageless in the same draconic way as the LeDoux family. Including me."

It was silent in the torturing chamber.

"So you mean, the only chance that we have in order to survive is to flee?"

"Yes. Or to find an ancient grimoire with a spell to murder them."

My heart pounded against my chest and I didn't even know why. "Are you serious? Something like that exists? And where is it?"

"That's the point." Thorne took a deep breath. "I don't know. Come on, Sparrow. We don't have time for these tales now." He opened the door to the hallway and I followed him through the Manor.

After some time, Thorne stopped abruptly and I ran into him. "What–"

"Shush!" He raised his hand. "I think I heard steps."

"Steps? That means we aren't alone!"

"I'm not sure. Could've been the wind. But we'd better hurry!"

Goosebumps covered my skin as we hasted on. I expected some shady figure to leap at us from every corner, but nothing happened.

We reached the dressing room and closed the door behind us.

I took a deep breath – and almost choked on my own saliva when a loud boom came from the other side of the door. Someone cursed and Thorne and I exchanged a terrified look, before simultaneously scurrying between the vast dresses.

Holding my breath, I pressed my back against Thorne's, hoping that no part of me would peek out from somewhere between the dress fabrics.

The door opened with a loud creak and heavy steps entered, heels clacking on the stone floor.

"You were mistaken," a male voice said. *Thill.*

"Idiot, I heard them talking!" *Estelle.* "They came in through the tunnel from the graveyard to the torturing chamber!"

"They are in South Farringdon, forgot that?"

"And what if they aren't there?"

"How would they have gotten rid of the wristbands? And even if, what should they be looking for here? Clothes? Estelle, you are paranoid."

"And you are an idiot." The heavier steps left the room.

A sigh, then a whisper. "I know you are here somewhere!" Estelle left the room as well and slammed the door, then it was silent.

For a solid five minutes, we remained on the floor, back to back, fearing that Estelle would return any moment.

When nothing happened, we finally crawled out of the pile of dresses.

"I'm not going to do this again," I said, pointing to the dresses. "It was terrible for fighting and fleeing. I'll wear a suit this time."

"Sounds, uh, reasonable." Thorne frowned and walked over to the suits. "But you need to cover your face somehow. A girl in a suit is really suspicious. I have some fake glasses up in my room from the disguise carnival party at school last year."

"Great, I'll get them together with my backpack later! Let's now take those things and run!"

Thorne sighed and grabbed three Victorian suits, fitting shoes and hats from the shelves. Somewhere between the dresses, I found the old clothing that we had left here last year, and I decided to take it with me, because – why not?

But when I tried to open the door, it was locked.

"What's up?" Thorne asked, a worried look in his face.

"We are locked in. Estelle must have locked the door to make sure we can't escape, in case we were here."

"Fuck it."

"No. I'm asexual."

"Sparrow!" Thorne shook his head. "No time for stupid jokes! We have a literal problem here!"

"We don't," I replied. "There's a *window*, idiot."

"Oh." Thorne turned around. "I remember when you jumped out of the window of the school together with me and said you'd never again do that!"

"Well, in that case you'll have to jump alone while I fly." I rolled my eyes with a deep sigh. "Thorne, we are on the freaking *ground floor!*"

THE OPERA
Sparrow

Ten minutes later, I flew up to Thorne's room, while he was watching me from behind the trees around the Manor.

I grabbed the backpack from below the bed, crammed the old clothing into it and rummaged through Thorne's drawers to find the glasses. Between school stuff and pencil sketches, I finally found them and put them in the backpack before leaving the room again.

I landed next to Thorne, but when I wanted to turn away and haste back down towards the village, he held me back. "I could just, you know, change my appearance to make it harder for them to recognise me!"

"Genius idea," I said, not sure if I meant it as sarcastically as I had said it. Shapeshifting might help, but the LeDouxes had recognised him as their lost son at the rite, no matter his appearance, so I wasn't sure if they could be tricked this time. "I mean, you could definitely try."

Thorne nodded and his body blurred in front of my eyes to a mess of colours. It wasn't the first time I had watched him change his appearance – last year at the rite, he'd become me – but it was the first time I witnessed it this closely.

It took only seconds until the blurring stopped and Thorne had turned into a random stranger with messy red hair, freckles and a round, pale face. His whole body had become taller and somewhat more muscular and once again, I wondered what Thorne *really* looked like – the boy who had been born as Phoenix Kyril LeDoux and had been known by that name for about 200 years. However, I knew that Thorne hated to talk about this period of his life, and I wondered whether he had forgotten, repressed the memories of his former self and appearance.

"We should go back to Cecily," the boy next to me said and I shivered. Even his voice sounded different, more adult-like.

The sun was already setting as we walked over the cobblestone roads and I realised that I had no idea when this event would take place. Cecily hadn't given us any information at all.

$$\approx \text{ 🕷 } \ll$$

When we reached the hotel room, Cecily was alone. She didn't even comment on Thorne's new appearance. For some reason, she seemed to know about his powers. I couldn't remember whether we had ever told her in one of those conversations we had had with her when she offered coffee and cookies in exchange for some gossip of our past at White Lilies.

Cecily gave us a serious look and explained, "Jasmine said she doesn't want to help you. She took the train home ten minutes ago."

Even though I couldn't hold it against her, I was disappointed. She just left us. Didn't feel the need to help us. Nothing. Again.

"But that doesn't matter," Cecily went on, "because we'll be less suspicious when we're with less people. By the way, did you get your clothing? The event will start in fifteen minutes!"

"Yes!" Thorne pointed to the suits that he had put on the table. "Sparrow decided on a suit, in case we have to fight."

"A suit?" Cecily frowned. "I hope you won't be too suspicious."

"I brought fake glasses," I replied. "That has to help somehow. So, we should probably hurry now, shouldn't we?"

She sighed. "Alright. Let's meet in five minutes in the foyer of the hotel."

After she left the room, Thorne and I got dressed in the Victorian suits. I hid my long hair under the top hat and put on the glasses. My eyes needed some time to get used to the unfamiliar view through the glass, but then I was ready to go.

"Sparrow," Thorne said as he put his hands on my shoulders. "Whatever may happen there, I will help you fight for your Mum. I know what she means to you, and she would make a great mother-in-law. I won't let her or you die in the hands of the Wicked Magicians."

"Thank you." I forced a smile upon my lips. Sometimes, there were words with more weight than a simple "I love you", even though they meant the same. And this was a perfect example.

"Let's go." Thorne let his hands slide from my shoulders and he walked over to my backpack to get the weapons. He had said they weren't useful against the LeDouxes, but they would work on the others.

He handed me the pistol, which I reluctantly shoved into my belt.

Then, he took a dagger out of his jeans that still lay on the bed – "Stole this from the torture chamber" – and hid it in the inner pocket of his suit. Inexperienced with suits and their possibilities to hide weapons, I just copied his move and after exchanging another look, we left the hotel room.

Cecily was already waiting in the foyer, wearing a blood red dress and a huge hat. "I have to warn you, kids. Do you have any weapons? They will check you for anything that looks like you could use it to fight."

"Weapons?" Thorne gave me an insecure look.

"I'm serious," Cecily said. "If they check you and find any weapons, you won't even get inside the opera! They'll kick you out before you can even start an argument!"

"Alright." I removed the dagger from my suit pocket and the pistol from my belt, taking the dagger that Thorne handed me as well. "I'll just bring the stuff back to our room, alright?"

"Sure. But hurry." Cecily tapped on the pocket watch she had taken from her handbag.

I nodded and ran upstairs. Under no circumstances would I go into that building without a weapon. I had promised Mum to use the pistol when it was necessary, so I would do so.

The only possibility that I saw in this moment was hiding it in my shoe. Unlike feminine boots, the shoes I was wearing now didn't have a bootleg to smuggle things, so I hoped the incredibly long trousers would cover up that I just tucked the pistol barrel into the shoe.

For a moment, I thought about putting the dagger in the other shoe, but the risk of injuring myself was bigger than the chance of using it, so I put it back into my backpack and returned to Cecily and Thorne.

"Remember, you aren't Thorne Fox and Sparrow Morrigane anymore, right?" Cecily said after giving me a harsh look for taking so long. She led us outside through the old streets.

"No?" Thorne frowned. "So you're telling us that we have to get used to fake names, literally five minutes before going to this event?"

"Yes, Franklin and Levi."

"Who is who?" I asked, almost stumbling over a huge cobblestone on the ground.

"Decide yourself."

Thorne sighed. "I'm Levi. What about my last name?"

"Wright. You are brothers," Cecily decided. "My nephews."

"Great."

And then, the huge opera was right in front of us.

Cecily smiled. "Let's go!"

Two huge figures in long coats stood in front of the main door, their cold eyes scanning each of us when we came closer.

"They belong with me, Sirs. My nephews Levi and Franklin," Cecily said.

"And you are?"

"Cecily Williams. The double agent."

"Ah yes? We've been told to not let you in." The taller man crossed his arms.

Cecily's confident façade shattered for a moment and she frowned in confusion, then she looked up again.

"Alright. Would you still let my nephews into the opera?"

"No. And we don't have any information about you bringing any family members, do we?" The shorter man looked up to his colleague.

"No." The other one shook his head.

"Alright. Then we have to give up. Say hello to the LeDouxes from me." Cecily sighed and walked away.

"You're not really giving up, are you?" Sparrow and I followed her into another street.

"Obviously not. Let's use the side entrance." Cecily led us to the backdoor of the opera, looked around and opened it. Within seconds, she disappeared into the darkness and Sparrow and I hurried to follow her.

It took a moment for my eyes to get used to the darkness, and Sparrow disappeared completely. I wasn't sure if she just struggled to control her powers in this moment or if she did it intentionally.

Cecily led us through a sinister hallway, past the dressing room, the costume wardrobe and some other rooms that I didn't know what they were for, and then she opened another door and we stood right in the middle of the opera.

The whole room wasn't too large, nothing like the huge operas in cities like London, but it was still impressive. Murmuring echoes sounded from the people who were standing on the upper tiers, sitting down here in the auditorium or waiting in the lines on the wall left of the stage, where a cold buffet was presented on overly full tables. I could spot small salads, sandwiches, cups of tea and other things you could expect for an afternoon tea party.

It wasn't afternoon anymore, but the LeDouxes assumingly didn't want to bring a full dinner menu.

"Can we get something to eat?" Sparrow asked.

"We'd better," Cecily said. "As you can see, everybody has something to eat. It seems as if that is a special manner here and we'd be impolite – and suspicious – if we wouldn't join."

So we made our way through the crowded auditorium to get to the other side of the room. Nobody had taken special notice of us yet, but still my heart pounded against my chest. I knew some of the guests from the rites! Seemed like the LeDouxes hadn't only invited the new Victorians from White Lilies Creek...

Even though many of the rite participants didn't even know the appearance of Thorne Fox, only the one of Phoenix Kyril LeDoux, and even though I currently didn't look anything like either of them, I still felt like somebody could tap my shoulder and call my name any second.

I took a deep breath and reassured myself: Nobody would recognise me.

Cecily handed me and Sparrow a bowl of salad and one sandwich each. She also picked some up for herself before we took a seat in one of the front rows.

Eating and talking about irrelevant things, we waited for the event to start.

Eventually, the gas lamps were turned off and an obscure atmosphere filled the room.

Rosary LeDoux entered the stage and the show began.

WELCOME TO THE FREAK SHOW
Thorne

"**A** warm welcome to my guests up there on the tiers, and another warm welcome to my friends and allies down here in the auditorium!" Rosary's oddly pleasant voice echoed through the room.

It was silent now, silent as the grave.

Why exactly had Cecily brought us here? Why hadn't we looked for Nevada backstage?

"I guess you know why you are here." Her voice became harsher. "If you don't know, I ask you to leave now and tell nobody about this gathering."

It was still silent. Nobody stood up. Everybody just gazed at Rosary.

"Good." She nodded. "You all received leaflets at some point in the last days. Your invitations to this gathering. I don't know what made you appear here – curiosity, or real interest in what we are doing here. Either way, I ask you to not tell anybody about it. In your own interest. You don't want to know what will happen to you if you tell someone."

Some people in the back exchanged quiet whispers, but were silent again as soon as Rosary's gaze hit them.

"You probably also know that everything that happens here is related to magic. Outside parties call us Wicked Magicians, but we as the LeDoux family and our friends do not identify as Wicked Magicians. We are our own group and we call ourselves Eternal Magicians. We are immortal. You probably know that as well – from all the media articles of last year's Summer Solstice. You will have exactly five minutes for your last chance to leave. If you don't leave, you will be a part of this. Irrevocably."

Now, some people in the back stood up, their clothes rustling as they hasted outside.

Then, it was silent again.

"Great," Rosary said. "Then it's time to demonstrate our magic ideologies. I ask on stage: Nevada and Sparrow Morrigane."

⌘ 🕷 ⌘

Sparrow

"**O**n this occasion, I also want to honour the effort that young Miss Morrigane has put into a disguise, but in vain," Rosary went on.

I stared at her, my hands trembling as her gaze met mine. How had she recognised me? How...?

"Come on," Cecily said and nudged me. "That's all a part of my plan! You will get on stage with your mother, and then you can flee together at a good moment. I'll work out how Thorne and I get out."

"You sure?" I got up with legs like pudding. She nodded and pushed me forward again. "It's all a part of my plan!"

I slowly walked over the red carpet leading to the stage. Rosary's malicious smile welcomed me as I stood there, all eyes on me, and they brought Mum out.

She didn't resist when Thill and Kyle dragged her on stage from the backstage area. She just stood there, glazed eyes, staring at the ground. Something inside of me broke when I saw her like that. The fighter. Lost.

"I will now demonstrate to you how blood potions work!"

Rosary reached for the rite dagger in her belt and Estelle and Clarisse brought a table with hundreds of vials, herb sachets and bowls on stage.

When exactly was the moment where I had to leave together with Mum?

My eyes searched for Cecily in the crowd, but her place was empty. Just like Thorne's.

I screamed when Rosary grabbed my wrist and cut my skin. Before I could fight back, she was already out of reach again and two strong hands grabbed my arms from behind. Clarisse. She lifted my bleeding right arm up high, so that everybody could see it.

"Do you all see this wound?" she yelled. "We're gonna heal it now!"

My heartbeat sped up. What was their plan, damnit? I couldn't even turn around, I just stared at the crowd and heard Rosary explaining some herbs and potions that she mixed together somewhere behind my back. And then I heard my Mum scream.

I spun around and kneed Clarisse in the stomach. She groaned in pain, but didn't back down. Holding my arms tighter, she pressed her knee on my spine and forced me to the ground.

"Let her go!" someone said in an incredibly calm voice.

"Cecily!" I lifted my head for a second. Our landlord stood at the edge of the stage, a pistol in her hands.

"Never, you traitor!" Clarisse crowed, pushing me harder to the ground. All my ribs ached and I expected them to break any second, when a shot was fired and the grip around my wrists and the pressure on my spine lessened within seconds.

Forcing myself to not turn around to look at Clarisse's immortal corpse, I got up from the floor, wiping the dust from my clothes. I had lost the top hat in the fight with Clarisse, and now my long hair curled on my shoulders. "Thank you, Cecily!"

"It was all part of my plan," she said, her pistol now switching between Estelle, who stood at the table, Rosary, who stood in front of Mum, a syringe in her hands, and Thill and Kyle, who held Mum's arms to prevent her from fleeing.

"You. Let her go." She spoke to Rosary, who stepped back when seeing the pistol. "And you." Her head turned to the two men. "Hold her tighter. This is my revenge. I am a Wicked Magician."

ॐ 🕷 ॐ

Jasmine

All eyes were on the stage, nobody paid mind to the figure in the dark cape that slowly sneaked towards the wicked scenery.

That figure that wasn't even supposed to be here.

Cecily had sent me home, had told me that Sparrow and Thorne would leave White Lilies Creek as well. But for some reason I hadn't believed her. Wouldn't they have told me that?

So I had decided to sneak into this event – just in time, as it seemed.

"You have me, so let her go!" Sparrow cried in that moment. "Wasn't that your plan all the time?"

"You misunderstood!" Cecily replied. "This was never about you, Sparrow Morrigane. Not about you or Jasmine or Thorne! This was always about Nemo! When I lived amongst the members of the Army in the war, to spy for my folks of Wicked Magicians, I had to watch her kill dozens of my beloved friends and family members!"

Okay, so she had tricked us. She wasn't on our side, and neither was she an ally spying in the Manor. She had always been on her own side. And the other things she had said? They were lies as well, weren't they?

Mrs. Morrigane and the Magic Army had fought against the Wicked Magicians, and for the rights of the Good Magicians and the Non-Magicians. What I had learned was that the Wicked Magicians hadn't even been human anymore. And all that Cecily said now heavily contradicted this.

"You murdered my friends and family," Cecily screamed in this moment. "And now I will murder you!"

"No! We want to torture her to punish her daughter," Rosary replied in anger.

"I want to kill her to punish her myself!" Cecily cried. "My plan was perfect! All I have done to bring her here was a part of my plan! So let me kill her now!"

Whack.

The heavy piece of wood hit her head and she fell to the ground without another sound. I lowered the club and pushed my hood back.

"Jasmine?" Sparrow stared at me in disbelief, while her Mum used the overall confusion to knock down the two men behind her. "Sparrow!" she screamed and Sparrow threw something over to her. I couldn't see what it was, but the LeDouxes backed down again.

"Run, girls!" Mrs. Morrigane screamed and Sparrow grabbed my hand and dragged me from the stage, through dark corridors. Steps behind us. And a loud knocking at the door there to the left.

"Thorne!" Sparrow stopped and ran to the door. "Jasmine, come over! Open the door!"

I ran to her. "You don't happen to have any wires with you?"

"Wires?" Sparrow stared at me. "No. Damn."

"Go away, girls!" Someone pushed me aside. Mrs. Morrigane. "Step back from the door, Thorne," she screamed and a shot was fired. The door slowly opened and Thorne stumbled outside, weird red strands in his dark hair and freckles fading slowly from his face. He was pale as a sheet. "Thanks, Nevada!"

"Don't thank me. We're not out of danger yet!" Mrs. Morrigane looked along the hallway, where the whole

LeDoux family – including Clarisse in a bloody dress – was running towards us.

"Come on!" She dragged us on, further through the dark corridors, and then, eventually, outside in a nightly Victorian street, illuminated by nothing but gas lamps and the full moon.

Mrs. Morrigane nudged me to run on. "To the hotel room!"

NEMO
Sparrow

Eventually, we sat in the comfortable hotel room around the dinner table, ignoring the loud pounding on the door.

We had locked the door and put a chair under the doorknob to latch it, so we were technically safe.

Rain hadn't left my shoulder since we arrived – he had certainly missed me.

"What happened in the last few minutes?" Thorne asked in an unusual quiet voice. He had entirely changed his appearance back to the way I knew him.

"Rosary hurt Sparrow and me, for a rite demonstration. And Cecily wanted to murder me for my sins in the war because she actually is a Wicked Magician," Mum replied.

"But you haven't committed any sins," I replied, my voice shaking.

"Well, I'm not so sure anymore." She gave me a grave look. "Cecily has said some things that made me think. And I will need some more information for the future. But for now, let's travel back home tomorrow, early in the morning. Thorne and Sparrow, you should move back to our house for now. I won't let you live in the same house as Cecily anymore, obviously. And you too, Jasmine, if you don't want to live with your parents for whatever reason."

Jasmine let out an uncertain sigh, while Thorne nodded, "Alright, thank you."

"Also – when I spied around in White Lilies Manor, I found something." Mum gave Jasmine a silvery necklace with a small pendant – Jasmine's full name was engraved in it.

"Thank you, Mrs. Morrigane," Jasmine said in a hoarse voice.

Mum took a deep breath. "Call me Nemo. We're at war again."

LIST OF IMPORTANT CHARACTERS

Sparrow Morrigane – Thorne's girlfriend; a sacrifice of the LeDouxes who escaped last minute; daughter of Nevada and Mortimer.

Thorne Fox – Sparrow's boyfriend; has also been a sacrifice of the LeDoux family who barely managed to escape; also the son of Rosary and Kyle.

Jasmine DeLuna – isn't she dead...?

Nevada Morrigane – Sparrow's mother; an ex-warrior and now a police woman; also known as Nemo.

Mortimer Morrigane – Sparrow's father; a vet.

Cecily Williams – the landlady of Thorne and Sparrow; also has a secret...

Rosary LeDoux – some sort of leader of the LeDoux family clan

Clarisse LeDoux – mother of Kyle and Estelle; actually the main leader of the clan

Thill & Estelle LeDoux – members of the LeDoux family

Kyle LeDoux – husband of Rosary LeDoux; father of Ethan and Thorne

Ethan LeDoux – son of Rosary and Kyle and brother of Thorne; is a baby

Rain – unicorn squirrel buddy of Sparrow

THANKS

Thank you to all my friends on Instagram who helped me develop the plot and characters, gave me advice for the cover designs and for an appropriate price for this book.

A very special thanks goes to my friend, alpha & beta reader and platonic wife Mirthe. Without you, White Lilies Creek wouldn't be the same, and I really enjoyed the iconic comment threads <3

Another Thank You goes to you as the reader. Your support means the world to me!

THE AUTHOR & OTHER BOOKS BY HER

The author Janina Raven is a 16-year-old German girl.

She has been writing since her early childhood and besides that, she also likes drawing, photography, graphic design, and listening to music.

In 2020 she published a novel and novella in German, which are called "Rebel School" and "Tungldraumur", as well as "White Lilies Manor", the first book of the White Lilies Trilogy.

She also appreciates book reviews on amazon or wherever you bought this book :)

Contact me: Instagram - @janina.raven.writing
Read more of my work: Wattpad - @janinaraven
Buy my merch: Redbubble - Raven&Duck